© of the american edition :
Editions Fleurus, Paris, 1997
ISBN : 0-7651-9188-1
All rights reserved. No part of this publication may be
produced, stored in a retrieval system or transmitted
in any form by any means electronic, mechanical,
photocopying or otherwise without obtaining written
permission of the copyright owner.
© Editions Fleurus, Paris, 1992 for the original edition
Title of the french edition :
Alice racontée aux enfants
English translation by Translate-A-Book, a division
of Transedition Limited, Oxford, England
Printed in Italy
Distributor in the USA : SMITHMARK Publishers Inc
115 west 18th street, New York NY 10011
Distributor in Canada : Prologue Inc
1650 Bd Lionel Bertrand, Boisbriand, Québec J7H4N7

ALICE
IN WONDERLAND

LEWIS CARROLL

ILLUSTRATED BY: MONIQUE GORDE

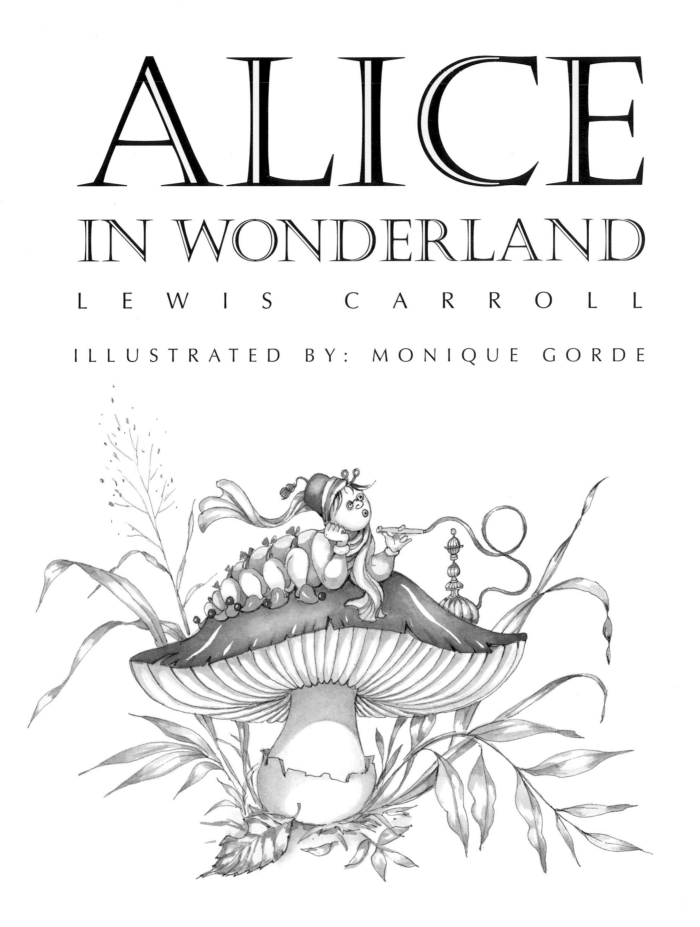

FLEURUS

CHAPTER ONE

THE WHITE RABBIT

It was a hot, sunny day and Alice was tired of having nothing to do. While her sister sat under the shade of a tall tree, reading her book, Alice lay down in the long grass and yawned.

The sun was making her feel very sleepy and stupid, so when a White Rabbit with pink eyes ran past, she didn't take much notice.

She wasn't even very surprised when the Rabbit stopped just in front of her and began talking to himself.

"Oh dear! Oh dear! I shall be late!" he muttered, pulling a large watch out of his waistcoat pocket and staring at it. Then he rushed off again.

That made Alice sit up straight.

"How very strange!" she said. "I've never seen a Rabbit with a pocket watch before."

She suddenly realized just how unusual the Rabbit was, for he not only had a pocket watch, but a pocket to keep it in. Indeed, he was dressed from head to toe in a beautiful suit of clothes!

Alice leapt to her feet.

"I wonder where he is going," she said. "And why is he late? I really must find out."

Forgetting how sleepy she had been, Alice ran off after the rabbit as fast as she could. She was just in time to see him disappear down a large rabbit hole under the hedge at the edge of the field.

Without stopping to think about where it might lead, Alice jumped down after him.

The next moment, Alice found herself falling down what seemed to be a very deep well. She wasn't frightened because she was falling very slowly and had plenty of time to look around her.

There was a lot to see, for the walls were covered with pictures and maps. There were also brightly painted cupboards and shelves filled with books and china jars. But when Alice looked down, it was too dark to see how far it was to the bottom.

"Perhaps I'm falling right through the earth," she said to herself. "Maybe I'll come out the other end and find everybody is upside down."

Down, down, down went Alice. She was just wondering if the journey would ever end when suddenly – thump! – down she came on a heap of sticks and dry leaves. The fall was over and Alice wasn't hurt a bit!

Alice jumped to her feet. In front of her was a long tunnel, and at the far end she could see the White Rabbit.

"Oh, my ears and whiskers, how late it's getting," she heard him say as he turned the corner.

There was not a moment to lose and so Alice ran to catch up with the Rabbit.

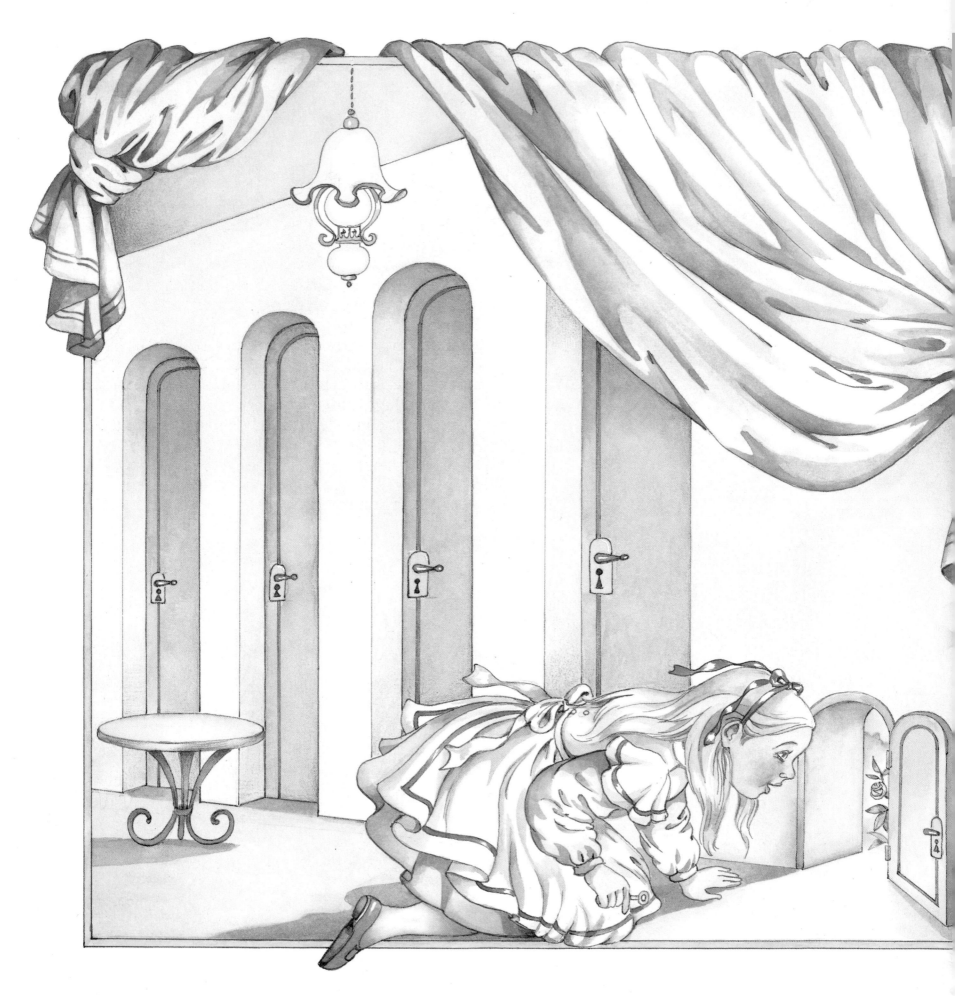

CHAPTER TWO

HOW ALICE BECAME BIG

When Alice turned the corner, she found herself in a large room surrounded by doors. There was no sign of the White Rabbit and, when Alice tried to open the doors, she found they were all locked.

Suddenly she came across a glass table with a tiny golden key on it. At first Alice thought it must open one of the doors, but it was far too small to fit any of the locks. Then, behind a curtain, she noticed a little door she hadn't seen before.

Kneeling down, Alice tried the key in the lock. To her great delight it fitted, and she pulled open the door. When she looked through the opening, Alice saw that it led to the loveliest garden she had ever seen. If she had been the size of a mouse she could have run outside at once. But, though she tried and tried, she couldn't even fit her head through the door. She was just too big.

Sighing, Alice locked the door once more and replaced the key on the glass table.

To her surprise, Alice found a little bottle on the table. She was sure it hadn't been there before, so she picked it up and read the label.

"Drink me," she read.

Alice carefully tasted what was inside. It tasted delicious, so she drank it down in one gulp. Then a most unusual thing happened – Alice began to get smaller. It was a strange feeling.

When she was about the size of a doll, Alice stopped shrinking.

"Now I shall be able to go into the wonderful garden," she laughed, running to the door.

But it was no use – the door was locked and Alice had left the tiny key on the glass table top, which was now far, far too high up for her to reach.

Almost crying, Alice sat down under the table and wondered what to do. Then she found a little box on the floor next to her. Inside she found a little cake with the words 'Eat me' written on it in currants.

Of course, Alice ate it all up. At once, she began to grow taller. She grew and grew, and then she grew some more. She didn't stop until her head hit the ceiling.

CHAPTER THREE

THE POOL OF TEARS

As soon as Alice stopped growing, she hurried to the little door once more. But of course, she was now too big to go through it. Indeed, she was far worse off than before. If she lay down on the floor, she could just about look through the door with one eye.

When Alice realized just how hopeless it was, she sat down in the corner of the room and began to cry.

She cried and cried. Although she told herself harshly that crying would not help, she just couldn't stop. The tears ran down her face and soon there was a large pool on the floor all around her.

Suddenly Alice heard footsteps coming toward her. It was the White Rabbit, still splendidly dressed and carrying a pair of white leather gloves and a fan.

"Oh, the Duchess, the Duchess!" she heard him mutter. "She will be so furious if I've kept her waiting."

The Rabbit didn't seem to notice Alice, but she was very relieved to see him so she decided to ask him for help.

"Please Sir…" she began, but before she could say any more the Rabbit jumped into the air with fright. Dropping his gloves and fan, he ran off as fast as he could.

"Oh, how strange everything is today!" cried Alice, picking them up. "I wonder what will happen next."

Alice was feeling quite hot, so she began to fan herself with the little fan.

"I must have frightened the White Rabbit because I am so large," she thought to herself while she fanned. "Oh dear, I wonder if I'll ever be the right size again."

Just then Alice noticed that she had put on one of the Rabbit's gloves.

"How can I have done that?" she wondered. "I must be shrinking."

Alice had shrunk to the size of a mouse before she discovered that it was the fan making her grow small. She dropped it quickly before she disappeared altogether! Then she ran off to find the door to the garden.

The next moment her foot slipped and – splash! – she was up to her chin in salt water. At first she thought that she had somehow fallen into the sea, but then she realized that it was the pool of tears she had cried when she'd been big.

"I *wish* I hadn't cried so much!" sighed Alice, starting to swim.

A little way off, Alice heard another creature splashing around in the water. Swimming closer, she saw that it was a Mouse that must have fallen in too.

At first the Mouse was frightened of Alice, but after a while they began swimming together until they finally reached the edge of the sea of tears and found dry land.

CHAPTER FOUR

THE CAUCUS RACE

There was a crowd of strange birds and animals gathered at the edge of the pool when the Mouse and Alice arrived. There were birds with bedraggled feathers and animals with their fur clinging to them, and they were all dripping wet, unhappy and uncomfortable. The first thing they wanted to do was to get dry again.

This caused quite an argument, for they all had different ideas about how to go about this.

"We shall have a Caucus Race," declared the Dodo finally. He was the largest of the birds there and obviously thought he was in charge.

"What is a Caucus Race?" asked Alice.

The Dodo said that the best way to explain it was to do it and he began marking out the race course in a sort of circle. Then he told all the creatures to stand around the course, here and there, and the race could begin.

And so it did – but since everyone began running whenever they liked, and stopped running whenever they liked, it wasn't easy to know when the race was over. However, in about half an hour, when everyone had raced round and round several times, and everyone was dry, the Dodo cried, "The Race is over!"

CHAPTER FIVE

BILL THE LIZARD

Very soon all the birds and animals went away and Alice was left on her own once more. However, she soon heard footsteps and, looking up, she saw the White Rabbit approaching again. He appeared to be looking for something. So, being a thoughtful girl, Alice leaped up to help him.

However, when the Rabbit saw Alice, he mistook her for his maid!

"Marianne, what are you doing here?" he cried. "Go home at once and fetch me a pair of gloves and a fan. Quick now, or I shall be late for the Duchess."

Alice was so surprised that she ran off at once.

"Though it seems very strange to be taking orders from a rabbit," she thought as she went.

She soon arrived at a neat little house that she was sure must belong to the White Rabbit. Luckily the front door was open. Alice went inside and ran straight upstairs, hoping that she wouldn't meet the real Marianne.

At the top of the stairs she found the White Rabbit's bedroom. There, on a table near the window, she found a fan and a pair of white gloves, just as she had hoped she would. She picked them up and was just about to leave when she saw that there was also a small bottle on the table.

"I know something interesting is sure to happen whenever I eat or drink anything," said Alice, picking up the bottle. "So I'll just see what this bottle does. I hope it'll make me grow large again, for I'm getting tired of being so small."

It did make her grow – and much sooner than she expected! She grew so fast that she soon filled the house completely, from roof to floor. When the White Rabbit came to find out where she was, he couldn't get in.

A few moments later, Alice heard whispering outside the window. The White Rabbit was telling Bill the Lizard to climb down the chimney to see why the door wouldn't open.

Now, Alice's foot was stuck in the fireplace. When she heard the creature scrambling down the chimney, she gave a little kick and sent Bill flying up into the air!

Then Alice felt some pebbles fly in through the window and hit her on the face. She was about to call out when she noticed the pebbles were turning into little cakes.

"Well, I surely can't get any bigger," she thought. "So perhaps they will make me small again."

CHAPTER SIX

THE ENORMOUS PUPPY

To Alice's relief, the little cakes *did* make her smaller. As soon as she was small enough, she ran out of the back door before the White Rabbit or Bill the Lizard noticed her.

"The first thing I've got to do," said Alice when she had stopped running, "is get back to my right size. And then I must find my way to that lovely garden."

She was about to set off again when a sharp bark above her head made her look up. An enormous puppy was looking down at her with big, round eyes.

Alice was very frightened. Hardly knowing what she was doing, she picked up a little stick and held it out to the puppy. The puppy yelped excitedly and rushed forward. Just in time, Alice dodged behind a large thistle to keep herself from being run over.

The puppy thought this was great fun, and charged at her again. This time Alice threw the stick as hard as she could. Then, while the puppy was rolling and tumbling after it, she ran off in the other direction as fast as she could go.

"It was a lovely, friendly puppy," she thought as she ran. "If only I had been the right size to play with it."

CHAPTER SEVEN

THE BLUE CATERPILLAR

When Alice stopped running, she looked around to see if there was anything she might eat or drink to make her grow again. Nearby there was a large mushroom and, standing on her tiptoes, Alice could see what was on the top of it.

To her great surprise, she saw a large blue Caterpillar sitting there. He was blowing smoke from a very strange pipe and Alice wasn't sure if he had noticed her standing there or not.

She was just about to turn and go away when the Caterpillar spoke.

"Who are you?" he said.

"I'm not quite sure," Alice replied. "I've been so many different sizes today, you see."

"I don't see," said the Caterpillar.

Alice tried to explain what had been happening to her.

"I don't really understand it myself," she said. "But being so many different sizes in a day is very confusing."

"It isn't," said the Caterpillar.

"Perhaps you haven't found it so yet," continued Alice, "but one day you'll turn into a chrysalis, and then into a butterfly, and that'll feel a bit strange, won't it?"

"Not a bit," said the Caterpillar.

"Well, I know it would feel strange to me," said Alice.

"To you?" said the Caterpillar. "*Who* are you?" Which brought them back to the beginning again.

Alice was starting to feel a little angry with the Caterpillar, so she turned away.

"Come back!" she heard him call. "What size do you want to be?"

"I would like to be a little bigger," replied Alice.

The Caterpillar got up, shook himself and crawled away, saying as he went, "One side of the mushroom will make you grow taller, and the other side will make you grow shorter."

Alice stretched out both her arms and broke off two pieces of the mushroom. Then she nibbled and nibbled, growing larger and smaller, until she became the size she wanted to be.

CHAPTER EIGHT

THE DUCHESS AND THE BABY

Once again Alice set off to find the lovely garden. She hadn't been gone long when she came upon a house. When no one came to answer her knock on the door, she let herself in.

The door opened onto a large kitchen, which was full of smoke. It was coming from a pot of soup on the fire, which was being stirred by a bad-tempered cook. She kept shaking a large pepper grinder into the soup and there was so much pepper floating in the air that Alice began to sneeze.

Sitting on a stool nursing a baby was a splendid woman who Alice decided must be the Duchess. The baby was sneezing and howling alternately without a moment's pause.

There was also a cat who was sitting in a basket on the floor. It wasn't sneezing, but it was grinning from ear to ear.

"Why does your cat grin like that?" asked Alice.

"It's a Cheshire Cat," said the Duchess, "and that's why. *Pig!*"

Alice jumped with surprise – but then she saw that the Duchess was calling the baby a pig and wasn't talking to her.

"I didn't know that Cheshire Cats always grinned," said Alice.

"You don't know much and that's a fact," nodded the Duchess.

CHAPTER NINE

THE CHESHIRE CAT

Alice carried on walking, wondering which way she should go next. She hadn't gone far when she was surprised to see the Cheshire Cat sitting on a bough of a tree above her. The Cat grinned at her.

"It *looks* friendly," she thought. But the Cat did have very long claws and a great many teeth, so she didn't go too close to it.

"Cheshire Puss," Alice began timidly, since she didn't know whether it would like the name. However, the Cat only grinned a little wider, so she went on. "Please would you tell me which way I should go now?"

"That depends where you want to go," the Cat replied.

"I don't much care where…" said Alice.

"Then it doesn't matter which way you go," interrupted the Cat.

"As long as I get somewhere," she finished.

"Oh, you're sure to do that, if you walk long enough," said the Cat.

Alice didn't find this very helpful, so she tried another question.

"What sort of people live around here?" she asked.

"The Hatter lives in that direction," said the Cat, waving his right paw, "and the March Hare lives that way." He waved his other paw, then added, "Visit whomever you like – they're both mad."

Then the Cat vanished.

Alice was beginning to get used to strange things happening, so its disappearance didn't startle her too much. However, before she could decide which way to go the Cat suddenly appeared again.

"By the way, what happened to the baby?" it asked.

"It turned into a pig," she answered.

"I thought it would," said the Cat, and vanished again.

Alice began walking towards the March Hare's house.

"I'm sure the March Hare will be more interesting to visit than the Hatter," she said to herself as she went.

She had hardly been walking for two minutes when the Cat appeared again.

"Did you say pig or fig?" asked the Cat.

"I said pig," replied Alice. "And I wish you wouldn't keep on appearing and vanishing so suddenly. You're making me very dizzy."

"All right," said the Cat. And this time it vanished very slowly, beginning with the end of its tail and ending with its grin. The grin stayed behind quite a long time after the rest of it had gone.

"Well! I've often seen a cat without a grin," thought Alice, "but I've never seen anything as strange as a grin without a cat!"

She was still wondering about it when she arrived at the March Hare's house.

CHAPTER TEN

THE MAD TEA PARTY

In the March Hare's garden there was a table set out under a tree, where the March Hare and the Hatter were having tea. A Dormouse was sitting between them, fast asleep, and the other two were using it as a cushion.

"That must be very uncomfortable," thought Alice, "but, because it's asleep, I suppose it doesn't mind."

The table was a large one, but when they saw Alice the March Hare and the Hatter called out, "No room! No room!"

"There's plenty of room," said Alice, and sat down in a big chair at the end of the table.

The Hatter took a large watch out of his pocket and looked at it. "This watch is two days wrong," he said to the March Hare. "I knew you shouldn't have cleaned it with butter."

"It was the best butter," said the March Hare.

"Yes, but some crumbs must have got in as well," sniffed the Hatter. Then he turned to Alice. "Why is a raven like a writing desk?" he asked.

Alice was glad that he'd begun to play a game, but she couldn't guess the answer to the riddle. "I don't know," she said. "Why is a raven like a writing desk?"

"I've no idea," replied the Hatter.

"Neither have I," added the March Hare.

"Then you shouldn't waste time by asking riddles that have no answer," said Alice wearily.

"If you knew Time as well as I do, you wouldn't talk about wasting it," said the Hatter.

"What do you mean?" asked Alice.

CHAPTER ELEVEN

THE QUEEN'S GARDEN

Alice could hardly believe it but finally, she found herself in the lovely garden she'd seen through the little door.

A large rose tree stood near the entrance of the garden. The roses growing on it were white, but three flat gardeners, who looked like playing cards, were busily painting them red.

"Look out, Five," one of them was saying. "You're splashing paint all over me."

Alice had never seen anything like it before.

"Excuse me," she asked. "Please can you tell me why you're painting those roses?"

The gardeners looked at her nervously.

"This should have been a red rose tree," admitted Two, "but we planted a white one by mistake. If the Queen finds out, she'll order our heads to be chopped off!"

While Two was speaking, Seven had been keeping a look-out. Now he threw his paintbrush into the air and called out, "The Queen! The Queen! She's coming now!"

Alice didn't really believe the Queen would order the gardeners' heads to be chopped off, but she felt sorry for them so she helped them to hide. Then she waited eagerly for the Queen to arrive.

It was a wonderful procession. First came ten soldiers, marching two by two. Then came ten courtiers, followed by ten royal children. Next came the guests, who were mostly kings and queens, although Alice also spotted the White Rabbit among them.

The Knave of Hearts came next, carrying the royal crown on a velvet cushion. Then, last of all, came the King and Queen of Hearts.

CHAPTER TWELVE

THE CROQUET MATCH

The Queen invited Alice to play a game of croquet. Usually croquet is played by hitting a ball with a wooden mallet through metal hoops stuck in the ground.

But *this* was a peculiar game. Instead of a mallet, Alice had to use a large pink flamingo; the balls were hedgehogs, and the hoops were the soldiers bent over to make arches.

Alice found it was a very difficult game. Her flamingo kept wriggling under her arm, and looking at her with sad eyes. Then, when she finally went to hit the ball, she found her hedgehog had crawled away.

"How nice to see you again," Alice was startled to hear someone say. Looking up, she saw that the Duchess had joined the game and was beaming at her with a big, friendly smile.

All the time they were playing, Alice could hear the Queen quarreling with the other players. Every few minutes the Queen yelled, "Off with his head!" or "Off with her head!" until Alice became quite upset.

When the Queen saw the Duchess she was furious.

"Leave now, or I shall chop off your head!" she ordered.

Finally there was no one left on the croquet field except the King, the Queen and Alice.

"Have you seen the Mock Turtle yet?" the Queen asked Alice.

"No," she replied. "I don't even know what a Mock Turtle is."

And so the Queen took Alice to meet the Mock Turtle who lived nearby with his friend the Griffin. Alice was a little worried when the Queen went off and left her with two such strange creatures, but they seemed to be friendly enough, although the Mock Turtle sobbed all the time.

First of all they told her about the lessons they had learned in school, which included Reeling and Writhing and Uglification. Alice had never heard of lessons like those before!

Then the Griffin and the Mock Turtle showed Alice a dance they knew. She was glad when they finished *that,* for they kept stepping on her toes as they passed by.

Finally the Mock Turtle sang her a sad song about green soup, while the tears ran down his face faster than ever.

Alice thanked her new friends and began to walk back to the Queen's garden, thinking that everything was now even stranger than before!

CHAPTER THIRTEEN

WHO STOLE THE TARTS?

When Alice got back to the garden, she found everyone was very busy. Somebody had stolen the tarts the Queen had made that morning and everyone was blaming the Knave, because of this poem:

The Queen of Hearts, she made some tarts
All on a summer's day.
The Knave of Hearts, he stole those tarts
And took them all away.

Alice thought it was a bit unfair to pick on the Knave just because of a poem, but the King and Queen of Hearts were determined to hold a trial in a court of law.

Alice sat down at the end of a long bench of creatures, which she guessed were the Jury. The King sat on his throne, next to the Queen. Alice realized that the King was also the Judge because he was wearing a wig under his crown.

In the middle of the court was a table with a large dish of tarts on it. The Knave of Hearts was being guarded by two soldiers and looked very sorry for himself.

"Call the first witness!" ordered the King.

The White Rabbit blew three blasts on his trumpet and called in the Hatter. Alice nearly laughed when she saw that he'd brought a cup of tea with him.

The Hatter was so nervous he kept spilling the tea and so he was sent away again.

As the White Rabbit called the next witness Alice decided that none of them knew how a real trial should be run. But, before she could speak, she felt a strange sensation which puzzled her a lot until she realized what was causing it – she was beginning to grow larger again!

"I wish you wouldn't squeeze so much," said the Dormouse, who was sitting next to her.

"I can't help it," replied Alice. "I'm growing."

"Well, you shouldn't grow so fast," said the Dormouse. "It's ridiculous!"

The trial continued and Alice was surprised to see that the next witness was the Duchess's cook. However, she was no more helpful than the Hatter and brought so much pepper with her that the whole court began sneezing! When they'd settled down again, the cook had disappeared.

The White Rabbit blew three more blasts on his trumpet and Alice wondered who the next witness would be. Imagine her surprise when the Rabbit called out "Alice!" at the top of his voice.

"Here!" she cried, leaping to her feet.

However, Alice had forgotten how large she had grown in the last few minutes. She jumped up in such a hurry that her skirt caught on the corner of the bench. The next thing she knew, the bench had tipped over, and all twelve members of the Jury were tipped off onto the floor.

The King and Queen were furious! The trial was stopped until Alice had picked up the creatures and set them back on the bench.

CHAPTER FOURTEEN

THE PACK OF CARDS

When the court had settled down again, the King continued with the trial.

"What do you know about this business?" he asked Alice.

"Nothing," she replied.

The King wrote something down in his notebook, called out, "Silence!" then read out loud from his book, "Rule Forty-Two. *All people more than a mile high must leave the court.*"

"I'm not a mile high," said Alice.

"You are," said the King.

"Nearly two miles," added the Queen.

"You just made up that rule," said Alice.

"It's the oldest rule in the book!" replied the King.

"Then it ought to be Number One!" said Alice quickly. The King couldn't think of a single answer.

Finally he shut his notebook and told the Jury to decide if the Knave was guilty or not guilty.

"No, no, no!" ordered the Queen fiercely. "First the Knave should be punished, then the Jury can decide if he's guilty or not."

"Nonsense!" cried Alice. "You can't have the punishment first!"

The Queen looked at Alice. "Off with her head!" she yelled.

Nobody moved.

"Who cares what you say," said Alice, who was no longer frightened of the Queen. "You're nothing but a pack of cards anyway."

At this the whole pack flew up into the air and came flying down on her head!

Alice was about to scream when – suddenly – she woke up! To her amazement she found herself back in the field with her sister. Alice had fallen asleep in the sun until some leaves fell onto her face and woke her.

"I've had such a strange dream!" cried Alice. And there we must leave her, telling her sister about all her wonderful adventures.